# THE CASE
# AGAINST THE WIND

DRAWINGS BY LEON SHTAINMETS

# THE CASE
# AGAINST THE WIND

## AND OTHER STORIES BY

# I. L. PERETZ

TRANSLATED AND ADAPTED BY
ESTHER HAUTZIG

MACMILLAN PUBLISHING CO., INC.
NEW YORK
COLLIER MACMILLAN PUBLISHERS
LONDON

Macmillan Publishing Co., Inc.
866 Third Avenue, New York, N.Y. 10022
Collier Macmillan Canada, Ltd.

Printed in the United States of America

1   2   3   4   5   6   7   8   9   10

Library of Congress Cataloging in Publication Data
Hautzig, Esther Rudomin.
The case against the wind, and other stories.
CONTENTS: The treasure.—The obsession with
clothes.—The seven good years. [etc.]
[1. Short stories]   I. Peretz, Isaac Loeb, 1851–1915.
Selected works. English. 1975.
II. Shtainmets, Leon.   III. Title.
PZ7.H289Cas     [Fic]     75–14193     ISBN 0–02–770990–6

FOR
RACHEL AND HENRY LISMAN
with abiding love and
admiration

# CONTENTS

# FOREWORD

Whenever I recall my childhood in Europe, I think of the stories my mother read to me in her melodious, low voice. And of all the stories that I can still hear in my heart and mind, those by Isaac Loeb Peretz are to me the sweetest and most lovely. Actually, I can hardly remember a time when I did not know Peretz's name, or hear his stories or read them to myself.

Isaac Loeb Peretz was born in 1852 in Zamosc, a small town in Poland. At the age of three he began attending Hebrew school, called a cheder in his time. His teachers at once recognized that he had an extraordinarily keen mind. When he was six, he began studying the Talmud, an enormously large collection of commentaries, debates, conclusions and discussions interpreting Jewish law.

As a young man Peretz began to read widely, not only in the fields of religion and Judaism, but in other subjects as well. He was given permission to use an old collection of books stored in the attic of a neighbor's house in Zamosc. Through the books he found there, he became well versed in science, law, history and in the writings of German, Russian and Polish writers. He taught himself to read these languages by using simple grammar books and dictionaries.

In the tradition of those days a marriage was arranged for Peretz when he was eighteen years old. His wife's name was Sarah Lichtenfeld. They had a son named Lucian, but the marriage was unhappy, and after five years they were divorced.

While he was married to Sarah, Peretz tried his hand at various business ventures, all of which failed. At the same time he also studied law. After his divorce he passed the law exams and was admitted to law practice in the year 1877.

In 1878 Peretz married again, this time very happily. His second wife's name was Helena Ringelheim. They lived in Zamosc, where for some ten years Peretz continued to practice law with great success.

Peretz had begun to write in Hebrew at a very young age, and he continued to do so for a number of years. In 1888, however, he began to write in Yiddish, and soon thereafter published his first important Yiddish work, the poem *Monish*. (Yiddish, by the way, is not the same as Jewish. To paraphrase something once said by the writer Maurice Samuel, to say that a Jew speaks Jewish would be about the same as saying that an Episcopalian speaks Episcopalian. Yiddish is a language; Jewish refers to a religion and nationality.)

Until Peretz and two of his contemporaries began to write in Yiddish, almost all writing for Jews was published in Hebrew, the language of the Holy Books. Although Jews prayed in Hebrew, many of them did not understand the words of the prayers, just as some Roman Catholics who prayed in Latin did not understand what they were saying. Only the well educated could write, read and speak Hebrew.

Peretz wanted to reach as many people as possible, so he wrote in Yiddish, the language that most Jews could read and understand. He wrote hundreds of poems, stories, plays, literary essays and articles on contemporary affairs. Some of his stories were serialized in newspapers and also published in very inexpensive penny-book editions which even poor people could sometimes afford to buy.

Peretz wrote honestly and poignantly about the feelings and the troubles of the common people. The heroes and heroines of his stories were peddlers, porters, seamstresses and woodcutters, as well as rabbis, saints and Biblical characters. Because miraculous, wonderful things often happened to these people, Peretz's readers were given hope too. Since anything was possible in Peretz's stories, couldn't anything be possible in real life as well?

In 1890 Peretz and his wife, Helena, moved from Zamosc to Warsaw, the capital of Poland. There he got a job with the social service section of the Jewish community organization. He held this job for the rest of his life. Peretz was also very active in the Jewish labor movement, and he wrote scathing articles about the appalling lot of Jews in eastern Europe. Anti-Semitism was rampant at that time, condoned and indeed encouraged by the governments. Jews were discriminated against in every way possible: they were denied jobs; most were forbidden to attend public schools or hold official positions in government; they were frequently attacked and beaten; their homes were regularly looted and destroyed.

The police followed Peretz's activities and his writings, and they were well aware of his criticism of the government's treatment of his fellow Jews. In 1899, while attending an illegal meeting where he read "Bontche the Silent" and some of his other works, Peretz was arrested. He spent several months in jail.

From the end of 1899 until his death nearly sixteen years later, Peretz devoted most of his free time to his writing. Since the income from this was very, very small, he could not afford to give up his job. Yet he found time not only to write an infinite variety of tales but also to advise and meet with many young Jewish writers who came to him for help and criticism of their work. To this day, he is considered the father of Yiddish literature.

After the First World War broke out in 1914, Peretz concentrated on helping Jewish children who were orphaned by it. He helped to found a home for these children and often visited them, playing with them and telling them stories. His happy face and laugh always cheered the frightened, lonely children. Peretz died at his desk in the year 1915, as he was writing a poem about the flight of a bird. One hundred thousand Jews attended his funeral in Warsaw.

Like I. L. Peretz, I was born in Poland, but fifteen years after Peretz died. The people walking in the marketplace and on the streets of my home town, Vilno, were very much like those about whom Peretz had written earlier.

The people in I. L. Peretz's stories are my oldest living friends. Few of my childhood friends from Vilno survived the Second World War in Europe, but Peretz's people—Bontche and Schmerrel, Basia Gittel and Tovye—are still with me, not a day older, still dear and true friends.

Peretz's people "traveled" with me to Siberia when I was ten years old, although I did not have a single Yiddish book in the five years we spent in that desolate part of the world. In Siberia my dream of Paradise often centered on having all the bread and all the sugar I could eat. My wish was not so far removed from Bontche's simple request of the Heavenly Court. Sometimes remembering Bontche eased my own misery.

Because Tovye and Sarah were such real people to me, not just fictional characters, I often hoped that perhaps I too would meet Elijah in the marketplace in Siberia! If miracles could happen to Tovye and Sarah, couldn't they happen to me?

When I returned to Poland after the war, I attended a Yiddish school that was named for I. L. Peretz. At the first postwar Chanukah party in my school, I recited from memory Peretz's first published work in Yiddish, the poem *Monish*. Even now, whenever I think of the time immediately after the Second World War, I think of Peretz and of his poem *Monish*, and of the school that was named for him, and of the Chanukah party—memories that often displace thoughts about bombed-out houses and exhausted people.

In this collection of ten stories, selected from the hundreds Peretz wrote, I have tried to give a sampling of his tales. These are some of my own favorites. Written at various periods during Peretz's life, they present a cross section of his work.

The stories and even this introduction include words that might be unfamiliar to some readers, but it seemed a shame to interrupt the stories with footnotes or lengthy explanations. Whenever you come across a word that you don't understand, look in the section called "Explanatory Notes" at the end of the book. If you would like to learn more about some of the subjects described in that section, check your library or bookstore. There are many fine books that explain Jewish holidays and customs more fully than I could or would want to in this book.

In translating from the Yiddish I found that some words and expressions are virtually untranslatable. Often I have had to approximate the meaning of the Yiddish words rather than give a literal translation. In retelling these tales in English, I have also had to make one or two of them shorter than they are in the original.

I do hope that the stories in this book will give you as much joy as they have given me over the years.

ESTHER HAUTZIG

# THE CASE
# AGAINST THE WIND

# THE TREASURE

To sleep on a hot July night in one little room, with a wife and eight children, was no pleasure, even on a Sabbath eve. Small wonder then that Schmerrel the woodcutter woke up, hot and breathless, in the middle of the night. He washed his fingertips in accordance with ritual, threw an old jacket over his shoulders and ran out of his inferno.

The streets were quiet. All the windows were shuttered. A tranquil star-studded sky hung over the sleeping town. Schmerrel felt that now, at last, he was alone with God, blessed be He. Schmerrel looked up to Heaven and said:

"Well, God of the Universe, this is a fine time for You to hear me and to bless me with a treasure out of all Thy treasures."

No sooner had Schmerrel said these words than a small flame flickered and ran ahead of him.

"This must be God's treasure for me! My wish was granted!"

Schmerrel wanted to run after the flame and catch it, but he remembered that running was forbidden on the Sabbath. So he walked slowly after the flame. But no matter how Schmerrel walked, the flame moved at the same speed. The distance between him and the flame never varied. As Schmerrel walked along, something in his soul tried to tempt him:

"Schmerrel, don't be a fool! Take off your jacket and catch the flame!"

He knew immediately, however, that this was the work of the Evil Spirit. He began to take off his jacket and seemed ready to throw it over the flame, but to spite the Evil Spirit, he slowed his pace. Schmerrel was happy to see that the flame also moved more slowly.

And so, walking leisurely after the flame, Schmerrel gradually reached the edge of town. The road twisted and turned over fields and meadows. The distance between him and the flame still never varied. Had he even tried to throw his jacket over the flame, he could not have reached it.

Meanwhile many thoughts went through his mind. If he could capture the treasure, he would not need to be a woodcutter when he grew old. Even now he was not as strong as he used to be. He would buy for his wife a seat in the women's section of the synagogue. Then she could sit down during Sabbath and holy days services. Now she had to stand, poor thing. He would get her a new dress, buy her pearls. The children would go to better schools. He would look for a bridegroom for his oldest daughter. It would be a good deed to catch the treasure!

Yet something stopped him.

"It must be the Evil Spirit which is tempting me. If the treasure isn't meant for me, then let it be so."

On a weekday, Schmerrel would not have hesitated to

run after the flame. If Yankl, his oldest son, were here, Yankl would have tried to catch the treasure, even on the Sabbath. His younger son was no better! He always made fun of his teachers. Children! Who knows what they will do? Did Schmerrel have time to look after his children? No, he had to cut and saw wood all day.

Schmerrel sighed and walked on. From time to time he looked up to Heaven and spoke:

"God Almighty! Whom do You wish to test here? Schmerrel the woodcutter? If You want to give, then give!"

Just then the flame moved more slowly than Schmerrel. At that very moment, too, he heard a dog's bark. It seemed to come from Visoki, the first village beyond town. In the early light of dawn, Schmerrel could see the whitewashed houses of the Visoki peasants. He realized that he had almost walked farther than was allowed on the Sabbath. He stopped.

"Yes, this is the place beyond which I may not walk. This is the Sabbath limit." Pointing at the flame, he said:

"You will not lead me astray. This is not God's work. God does not mock people. The Evil Spirit is making fun of me!"

Feeling angry at the Evil Spirit, Schmerrel whirled around, left the flame behind and walked back toward town. He decided to say nothing about any of this at home.

"First of all, they won't believe me. And second of all, if they do believe me, they will laugh at me. Anyway, what shall I boast of? The Lord of the Universe knows that I

5

have not broken the laws of Sabbath and that is quite enough.

"For all I know, my wife may even get angry that I did not try to catch the flame. The children surely will be angry—barefoot and ragged as they are, poor things. Why should I encourage them to break God's commandment to honor their father?"

No, Schmerrel would not let a word escape his lips. He would not even remind God of this night. If he, Schmerrel, had acted well, then God would remember it Himself.

"Money, after all, is here today and gone tomorrow. Money can even lead you astray!"

At last Schmerrel felt totally at peace. He wanted to sing to thank the Lord. He remembered the song, "Our Father," from his youth and began to sing, but became abashed and stopped. As he tried to recall a chant from the synagogue, he saw that the flame was once again in front of him. It was heading slowly toward town.

Again the distance between the flame and Schmerrel never varied. As the flame strolled, so strolled Schmerrel —both, it seemed, in honor of the Sabbath.

The sky was becoming pale, the stars were fading. On the eastern horizon the first rays of sun were slowly stretching into a crimson stream. The flame, meanwhile, turned in the direction of Schmerrel's street, toward his house. His door was open—he must have forgotten to close it. The flame went in. Schmerrel followed the flame and saw it creep under his bed. Everyone in his house was still asleep. Schmerrel tiptoed over to his bed, bent down and looked under it. Like a magic top, the flame spun round and round. Schmerrel took off his jacket and threw it over the spinning flame as the first rays of sun peeked into the room. No one heard him.

Schmerrel sat down on his bed. He vowed not to say a word about the treasure under his bed until the end of Sabbath. Otherwise, God forbid, the holy day might be profaned. His wife would not be able to contain her curiosity, his children even less so. They would want to count, to know how large the treasure was. Soon the secret would be out of the house, on the streets and maybe even in the synagogue. No one would pray, or say the blessings and the benedictions. He, Schmerrel, would cause transgressions not only in his own household, but in half the town as well. No, not even a whisper would escape his lips.

After Havdala, the final Sabbath prayer, Schmerrel bent down and looked under his bed. His jacket was still there. He removed it and found underneath it a big bag full of gold, more gold than he could even count.

Because of his piety, and his observance of the laws of Sabbath, Schmerrel the woodcutter had become a rich man. He lived out his days without a care in the world. But even in their great wealth and happiness, his wife often would reproach him:

"My God, how could you have had such a heart of stone? Not to have said a word to your own wife about the treasure! And I used to cry so bitterly when we did not have a penny in our house and I said my prayers."

Schmerrel, smiling, would comfort her by saying:

"Who knows, dear wife? Perhaps your prayers brought us this good fortune?"

# THE OBSESSION
# WITH CLOTHES

Basia Gittel lived many, many years ago in Schebrin. She was a good woman, from a fine family. Her husband was a Hassid named Elimelech. He was a tradesman who had to be away from home for long periods of time. His business was in far-away Leipsk, for there was much more trade there than in Schebrin. At least once a year Elimelech also went to Lublin to see a holy man, a tzaddik.

While her husband was away, the devil found ample time to tempt Basia Gittel. The devil knew, however, that she would not commit a really unspeakable sin. Basia Gittel was, after all, a pious soul. She read many Yiddish translations of the Holy Books and was devoted to doing charitable deeds.

The devil therefore decided to tempt Basia Gittel with a

lesser sin—an obsession for clothes and adornments. Since Elimelech was a wealthy man, he gave Basia Gittel a very generous allowance for housekeeping. That made it easier for her to fall into the devil's trap.

The devil, of course, did not come to her as his own true self. He disguised himself as her guardian angel and spoke to her with sweet and pious words. He claimed that he only wanted her to get new clothes and jewels for the sake of her soul, for the sake of Heaven.

"Passover, the holy festival in observance of the Exodus from Egypt, is coming. The Lord blessed you with all good things. Shouldn't you honor the holy festival by wearing a new dress? You will not only do honor, but perform a good deed, too! The dressmaker will make money for Passover, and you will welcome the holiday in clothes of joy. Isn't that so?"

Basia Gittel was impressed by the devil's words. She baked fewer matzoth for Passover, prepared a less elaborate Seder feast and gave less money to the poor. Then she ordered for herself an expensive gown with silver trimmings.

Shavuoth, the devil said, is also an important holiday. After all, it celebrates the giving of the Torah on Mount Sinai! So Basia Gittel bought a pearl necklace.

For Succoth, the gay autumn harvest feast, she got two shawls, and diamond earrings, too. She bought special finery for Rosh Hashanah, which was the beginning of a new year. Purim was a holiday as well, Chanukah not less so. There certainly was no shortage of holidays!

Then the devil said that Basia Gittel had to honor every Sabbath, for it was as holy as all the other holy days. So Basia Gittel bought new things to celebrate each Sabbath —a silk scarf, a ribbon, gloves. It was a good deed, too, the devil said, to dress up to welcome her husband when he returned home. A woman needed adornments to be pleasing in her husband's eyes.

As for jewels, the devil had additional advice. Rubies would assure her easy pregnancies. Emeralds would bring her good fortune. Sapphires would make her even wiser than she already was.

The devil was surely leading Basia Gittel on a slippery path! Her obsession grew more overpowering each day. When the devil saw that she was rolling downhill like a stone that had needed only a slight push, he stepped aside and let her continue to the bottom by herself.

Basia Gittel reduced her contributions to charity. She cut down on food for her children and herself. She engaged less costly tutors for her boys. She spent all she could for more clothes and jewels.

Still it was not enough. Basia Gittel let her servant girl go and made a list of breakages the servant had caused. She deducted the cost of these from the girl's wages, even though the girl protested that she had never broken anything.

Then Basia Gittel took in a poor orphan girl, a relative, to work for her. She told the girl that she could not pay her wages, but she promised that when the time would come for her to marry, she would give her many presents—

11

and even some of her own dresses. In the meantime Basia Gittel used what would have been the girl's wages to buy more clothes and adornments. Elimelech knew nothing about any of this, for he was almost constantly away.

Years passed by. Then one day it came to pass that Basia Gittel could not move her legs. She seemed healthy in all other ways. She ate well and slept well and looked well. There were no wounds or marks on her legs. But she could not stand or walk, and no medicines seemed to help.

Perhaps this strange illness came on to cure Basia Gittel's obsession? It seemed as if Heaven itself wanted to protect her. Since she stayed in bed all day, and did not go out either to the street or to the synagogue, what good were new clothes? So walls should see them?

Nevertheless, Basia Gittel's obsession was so powerful that she continued to buy new dresses. Several times a week she would order that all of her dresses and her jewels be spread out on chairs and benches by her bed. She would then lie in bed and look at them with satisfaction.

Once, when her dresses were spread out around her, Basia Gittel noticed that there were spots and stains on her most gorgeous silk and velvet gowns. In a few places they were even torn. She screamed and cried and carried on. All her neighbors rushed in to see what had happened. The neighbors said that none of them could be at fault; none of them would have worn her dresses. They talked it over with Basia Gittel and decided that only the orphan girl could be guilty. Quiet and meek though she was, only she could have dressed at night in her mistress's dresses and sneaked out of the house.

12

The girl did not confess, though she was scolded with words that should neither leave one's lips nor be written down. She was humiliated and beaten. The neighbors dragged her to the rabbi and told him that only she could have worn the dresses—only she! Didn't she look scrawny and thin? Yet she lived with a good kinswoman, a rich relative, who must have fed and cared for her well! It must be that she did not sleep at night and went to drink and dance in evil places.

The neighbors shaved the girl's head, so that she would appeal to no one. They chased her out of town and even threw stones at her. That was the custom in those days.

During all of that time Elimelech was not at home. He had gone to the holy man, the tzaddik, in Lublin, and he refused to leave until the tzaddik gave him a cure for Basia Gittel. The tzaddik had offered special prayers for her, but they did not help. Worse still, the tzaddik felt at times that his prayers were flung back at him from Heaven. He realized that his prayers met with Heavenly opposition, that some grave sin must be in the way.

"What is it?" he asked of Heaven a few times. He was not answered. "It must be an ugly matter, something that should not even soil my lips."

The tzaddik finally told Elimelech to go home and to return with Basia Gittel. The tzaddik was an expert at "reading" faces. He wished to examine Basia Gittel in person so that he could read what was written on her forehead.

Elimelech went home to Schebrin. He rented a large wagon and made a bed inside it for Basia Gittel. He hitched two horses to the wagon and started quickly for Lublin. In towns along the way, new horses were waiting to replace the ones that tired. Elimelech did not want to waste a minute on the road.

After their last stop for fresh horses, a heavy snow began to fall. Night came. There was no moon. There were no stars. Elimelech could not see the road and became lost in a deep forest. In those days the woods were dense. Tree branches grew together so closely that even during daylight it was dark. Robbers hid in those woods, and at night there was real danger. Though they were afraid of robbers, Elimelech and Basia Gittel decided to stop and wait for morning.

Suddenly, from afar, a little light appeared. The light grew larger. Then a second light appeared, and a third and fourth. Perhaps the lights came from an inn? Elimelech drove toward the lights. As they came nearer, they heard music and laughter. There must be dancing in the inn. Soon the inn appeared, its windows ablaze with lights. Perhaps rich landowners or Polish princes were giving a ball? Or perhaps it was a wedding feast? Surely it was better to find a gathering of merrymakers than to meet wild animals or robbers in the woods. As Elimelech and Basia Gittel came closer to the inn, they heard that the musicians were playing Jewish songs. A badchen, a merry-making jester, was entertaining the guests, making up verses and calling out wedding dances.

Elimelech trembled. He realized who these creatures were! They were devils who lurked in deep forests and celebrated mock weddings in desolate inns.

"Listen to me, Basia Gittel! We have fallen into evil hands. For Heaven's sake, remember! We must not answer their questions, nor accept their hospitality, nor take anything to eat or drink."

Basia Gittel lay in the wagon more dead than alive. She nodded her head. She knew. And she really did know of such goings-on. She had read about them in her Yiddish translations of the Holy Books.

The guests, the badchen and the musicians rushed out of the inn. They begged Elimelech and Basia Gittel to join the wedding feast. All the members of the wedding party urged them to join the fun. The badchen told more jokes; the music played. Servants carried out refreshments on silver platters and in crystal and gold goblets.

"Here! Make a blessing! Eat! Take! Enjoy!"

Elimelech and Basia Gittel did not say a word.

Suddenly Basia Gittel saw that the bride, the ladies in the bridal party and all the women guests wore her best velvet and silk gowns. The gowns were stained with food and drink, and they were even ripped in many places. Basia Gittel's heart nearly burst as she cried out:

"Thieves! Robbers! My dresses!"

Crying out nearly killed Basia Gittel. Elimelech whipped the horses and the wagon sped off to Lublin. Basia Gittel fainted many times on the way there. Her mouth became misshapen and she was completely helpless. Elimelech barely managed to get her to the tzaddik. The tzaddik realized immediately what had happened, but he could do nothing.

He told his followers to take heed and remember that

when a Jewish woman makes new clothes, she must distribute her old ones to the poor. In any case, a good woman must not make new dresses if she cannot wear them. When there are unused clothes hanging in the closet, evil spirits take them out and dance in them at their feasts and weddings.

When Basia Gittel heard these words, she said that she wished to die. Before her wish was granted, she begged for God's forgiveness, and the tzaddik promised her she would receive it. Just before her death she also told her husband about the orphan girl who had been accused so falsely. She held his hand and made him promise her that he would search for the girl and marry her.

Elimelech fulfilled her wish. After shivah, the seven days of mourning for Basia Gittel, he began to search for the orphan girl. He found her and later married her. She became a good mother to his and Basia Gittel's children.

Later she and Elimelech had children of their own. They raised them to study Holy Scriptures and lived to see them married and content.

All Jews should do as well.

# THE SÉVEN GOOD YEARS

Once upon a time, in Turbin, there lived a porter by the name of Tovye. He was very, very poor.

One Thursday afternoon, Tovye stood in the market-place and looked around for work. He hoped to earn a few cents for Sabbath, but all the stalls were empty. No one was buying anything and so no one there would need a porter.

Tovye lifted his eyes to Heaven:

"Please, dear God, see to it that at least on Sabbath we will not go hungry. See that my wife, Sarah, and our children have a happy Sabbath."

As Tovye was praying, he felt someone tugging him by his coattails, which were tucked under a rope around his hips. Tovye turned around and saw a stranger. The stranger was dressed like a hunter, with a feather in his hat and green trimmings on his jacket. The man spoke to Tovye in pure German:

"Listen, Tovye! I bring you good news. You have been given seven good years, years of luck and great fortune. You must choose when you want these seven years to come. If you wish, these good years will begin on this day. You will be a rich man even before the sun sets. You will be able to buy up all of Turbin and the surrounding lands. After the seven years, however, you will be very, very poor again. But if you prefer, the good years will come to you at the end of your life and you will be a rich man when you die."

The stranger was, in fact, Elijah the Prophet. As was his custom, he had come disguised, this time as a German hunter. But thinking that the stranger was an ordinary magician, Tovye replied:

"My dear sir, please leave me alone. I am so poor that I have nothing even for the Sabbath. I cannot pay you for your advice and efforts."

The stranger, however, persisted, and repeated his offer three times.

At last Tovye reconsidered.

"Well, dear sir, if you speak the truth and do not mock my poverty—and if you aren't by some chance crazy—then I will tell you something. On important matters I always consult with my wife, Sarah. I cannot give you an answer unless I discuss it with her first."

"Very well," said the stranger. "It is a good idea to consult with one's wife. Go and speak to her. I will wait for your answer."

Tovye looked around again, but there were still no customers in sight. What could he possibly lose? He would go home and speak with Sarah.

Tovye went to the outskirts of town, where his small mud hut stood by a nearly open field. It was summer, and the door was ajar. When Sarah saw him through the door she ran out joyfully to greet him. Perhaps he had earned some money for the Sabbath? Tovye told her quickly:

"No, Sarah, it was not God's will that I should earn money for the Sabbath. Instead a stranger spoke to me . . ."

And Tovye repeated the stranger's words to Sarah and told her of the promised years of plenty, and of the decision they had to make.

"When?" Tovye asked Sarah.

And Sarah immediately answered:

"Go, dear husband, and tell the stranger that you wish the good years to begin right now!"

"Why, Sarah?" Tovye asked, astonished. "After seven years we will be once more poor! After having great riches, won't it be much harder to be poor again?"

"Don't worry about the future, my dear friend. Take what you are offered now and thank the Lord for His blessings. We need the money *now* to pay for our children's education. The teachers sent them home from cheder because we could not pay the school! See, there they are, playing in the sand."

This news was enough to make Tovye run back to the stranger with a definite answer: He wanted the seven good years to begin immediately. The stranger seemed surprised.

"Consider carefully, Tovye. Today you are still strong. You can earn a living—sometimes more, sometimes less. But what will happen later, when you are old and do not have the strength to work?"

"Listen, dear stranger. My wife Sarah wants the good years to start right now. First of all, she says, 'Thank God for His gifts today, and do not worry about what's to come!' Secondly, our children were sent home from cheder because we could not pay for their education."

"If that is so, go home," answered the stranger. "You will be rich even before you get to your house."

Tovye wanted to ask more questions about the future, but the stranger vanished. Tovye decided to go home. When he came near his mud hut by the open field, he saw his children playing with sand. When he came closer he realized that they were playing not with sand but with pure gold.

The seven lucky years had begun!

Time flew and seven years sped quickly by. The stranger reappeared to Tovye. He met him in the marketplace, just as he had done seven years before. Tovye's old coattails were still tucked under a rope around his hips, and he still looked about for work.

"Well, Tovye, the seven lucky years are over. The gold in your yard will disappear. So will the gold in your house, and even the gold that you may have hidden away with neighbors."

"Tell this to my wife," Tovye replied. "She has been in charge of our wealth the last seven years."

The stranger and Tovye went to the edge of town and came to the same poor mud hut near the open field. They met Sarah by the door. She was as poorly dressed as she had been seven years before, but her face was happy.

"The seven years of plenty are over!" the stranger said.

"Listen, stranger!" Sarah replied. "We did not even begin to have years of plenty! We never considered the gold our own. Only what we earn with our hands is truly ours. Such wealth as came to us without the sweat of our brows and unasked was only entrusted to us by the Lord to keep for the poor. We used the gold only to pay for the children's education, to learn God's Torah. We used His gold only to learn His teachings, and for nothing else. If God, blessed be His Name, now has a better keeper for His gold, let Him take it and turn it over to that person."

The stranger, who was Elijah the Prophet, listened to Sarah's words and then vanished. He repeated Sarah's words to the Heavenly Court. The Court decreed that a better keeper for God's riches could not be found on all the earth, and the years of plenty continued for as long as Tovye and Sarah lived.

# REVEALED

Many years ago an old couple came to our village. Only God knew where Lemach and Genendel had come from. They came without children. Perhaps they had had children and lived to see them married? Perhaps, God forbid, their children had died? Perhaps they had never even had any children? Who knows?

Lemach and Genendel arrived in the afternoon. The first night they slept in the poorhouse. The next morning they went to Clay Street, where all the poor people lived, to look for a place to live. They found a kitchen with a dark alcove, and settled in. They unpacked the wooden box and two baskets in which they had brought their few belongings. They found straw and sacks to sleep on. Then they went in search of work.

Lemach, a small, quiet man with moist eyes and a high voice, joined a society of pious men who spent most of their time alone, reciting psalms. Soon he was much liked by all the members of this group.

Genendel, a big woman with hands and feet and voice like a man, took a stall in the marketplace and soon began to buy and sell things. Each day she shouldered her way through the marketplace and streets. Her booming voice could be heard all over the village. Lemach, who could earn no money, was almost never seen nor heard by anyone. He sat by a penny candle in his alcove and recited psalms all day.

The walls of the houses on Clay Street had cracks and holes. Neighbors could look and listen through the cracks. They were curious to know how a big, forceful woman like Genendel could get along with a quiet little man like Lemach. Beilke, the soldier's wife, lived next door to Lemach and Genendel. She watched them through the cracks and reported to the neighbors.

Beilke and the neighbors were astonished. At home Genendel was not a noisy, forceful person, but quiet and meek. She came home quietly in the afternoon. She made a fire and cooked potatoes, or something else, for supper. While the food was cooking, she stood quietly by the stove or knitted socks. From time to time she sent loving looks toward the alcove where Lemach studied.

When the food was ready, Genendel put out the fire, set the table and turned up the light in their oil lamp. Then she went over to the alcove and knocked gently on the door. When Lemach came out, she stood aside and let him pass.

The couple washed, Lemach said blessings, they ate and thanked God—all quietly. After dinner Lemach got up, smiled at Genendel and returned to the alcove. She too got up, stood awhile and looked at Lemach until he shut the alcove door. Then she lowered the light of the oil lamp and washed the dishes.

Beilke, the soldier's wife, imitated this so well that all the neighbors were doubled up with laughter.

Sometimes Genendel would have nothing with which to greet the Sabbath. Then she'd go over to the alcove door and tell Lemach, as if it were a shame or a sin, that this or that was lacking for the Sabbath.

"Perhaps you have something in your pockets?"

"No," Lemach would answer with a sweet smile, "I have nothing, but don't worry. God, our Father, will take care of us." Then he would return to reading psalms. Genendel would take his words to heart, and hope that as soon as she left the house, she would earn something for the Sabbath.

Beilke imitated this, too, and made the neighbors laugh. They even forgave her for not paying her rent. Who could throw Beilke out? A dark mood would descend on the whole house!

Genendel knew of Beilke's jokes and teasing. Whether she paid attention to them was anybody's guess, however, for she never said a word.

Once it came to pass that Genendel again had nothing to prepare for the Sabbath. She went over quietly to the alcove door and knocked three times. When Lemach did not come out, she became uneasy. She opened the door a crack, and saw that the usually dim alcove was flooded with light. In this bright light sat Lemach, absorbed in a Holy Book. He neither saw nor heard Genendel. Genendel quickly closed the door.

"I will not bother him," she murmured to herself. "Surely he knows anyway what I need to make the Sabbath meal."

They did have candles to light and bless, and challah for the bread-blessing. If worst came to worst, these would be enough. But so that the neighbors should not know how meager their Sabbath meal would be, she decided to light a fire in the oven. When she remembered that there was no firewood, Genendel did not despair. She pulled out the straw from her sleeping sack and made a fire. When the fire burned, she smiled.

"Let them look through the cracks!"

She grabbed some pots, filled them with water, and put them noisily into the oven. Again she smiled.

"Let them hear!"

Then, with a great flourish, Genendel went outside and folded her arms. Her Sabbath meal was cooking.

How did Lemach and Genendel spend that Friday night? What did they eat? How did Genendel feel, sitting at her table, knowing that the holes and crevices in their walls were filled with eyes and ears? How did she sleep all night on her empty sack?

During the night Genendel regretted her deception. She

realized that she had not really fooled her neighbors. She could hear whispers and snickers behind the walls. Beilke whispered to the neighbors, reminding them to send to Genendel the Sabbath gentile, who opened oven doors and did other tasks which were forbidden to Jews on Sabbath.

"Remember tomorrow. . . . Tomorrow remember to send the Sabbath gentile to open Genendel's oven!"

After Sabbath morning services in the synagogue, Genendel returned home. She found Beilke in her kitchen. Beilke's downcast eyes barely masked her glee. She held her hands behind her back, hiding something. Genendel's heart began to pound. She knew that her torture was beginning, but she did not forget what day it was and said:

"Good Sabbath."

"Good Sabbath, Genendel, and a good year to you, too. You do know why I am here, don't you?" Beilke asked sweetly.

Genendel's lips trembled but she did not answer. Beilke continued:

"Since my husband, Velvel, was lost, I do not prepare my own Sabbath meal. I eat a bite here and there. The neighbors are not always happy to share their food with me. But I know what a generous heart you have, Genendel! I heard how busy you were yesterday with your pots and pans. I am sure that God helped you to prepare a fine Sabbath meal, and I know that you will be glad to share it with me. I've even come to you with my own spoon."

Beilke took out the tin spoon from behind her back.

Genendel was about to admit the truth when the door opened and she heard Lemach say, "Good Sabbath!"

Lemach's sweet greeting was followed by someone else's "Good Sabbath!"

Lemach had brought along a guest from synagogue—an old man with a long white beard and glowing eyes.

"Good Sabbath and a good year to you," answered Genendel.

"You see, Genendel," Lemach said, "our guest spent a miserable Friday night in the home of misers. So today I brought him to our home."

The house spun around Genendel's head.

At that moment the door opened and the neighbors rushed in, pushing and laughing. They had brought along the Sabbath gentile!

That was more than she could bear. Genendel cried out:

"No! No!"

She ran over to her oven and would not let the Sabbath gentile touch it. At that moment a change came over Lemach. He seemed to have become tall, strong and forceful. In his sweet but now firm voice he said:

"You must have faith in God, Genendel! If not for our sake, then for the sake of our guest, and for the sake of Sabbath!"

The room became very quiet. No one spoke. Beilke got ready to run. Genendel moved away from the oven door. Lemach smiled and said to Beilke:

"Stay, woman, stay. If there is enough for us, there will be enough for everyone."

Beilke remained. Genendel trembled.

The Sabbath gentile opened the oven door. The delicious smell of beans and meat spread throughout the room, just as in the homes of very rich people.

Genendel and Lemach and their guests said blessings, sang hymns and enjoyed themselves.

Between hymns, Lemach turned to the old man and said:

"Dear guest, you see this woman, sitting here so quietly and nicely? She is always making jokes, laughing, imitating people . . ."

The color changed in Beilke's face, but Lemach smiled and continued:

"Perhaps you think, God forbid, that she is insolent? On the contrary, she is a modest Jewish daughter. What then? Poor thing, she is all alone. Her husband, Velvel the soldier, was lost in Russia. She tells jokes and ingratiates herself with people, and in return she gets some food. People permit her to dip her spoon into their bowls."

The old man asked Beilke about Velvel. It seems that he saw him in Vitebsk. . . . But that is quite another story.

# IF NOT STILL HIGHER

The Rabbi of Nemirov disappeared every morning during the days of Slichoth prayers. He could not be seen anywhere. He was not in the main synagogue. He was not in the two smaller houses of prayer. And he was definitely, absolutely, not at home. His door was always open. Whoever wished could walk in and out, for no one would ever steal from the Rabbi of Nemirov. His house was empty! Where, then, could the rabbi be?

Where *should* he be if not in Heaven? He certainly had enough to do there. His flock needed to make a living; they wanted peace, good health, happy marriages for their children. Who should help them if not their rabbi?

That's what the people of Nemirov had thought.

One day, however, a Jew from Lithuania came to town. Everyone knew that the Litvak—for that is what all

Jews from Lithuania were called—was well versed in the Talmud. The Litvak laughed at what the people of Nemirov thought. He quoted passages from the Holy Books which said that even Moses could not go to Heaven while he was alive; even he had to stop at least ten feet below Heaven. So who could argue with the Litvak's knowledge?

Where then *did* the rabbi go?

"Is it my business?" the Litvak said, and shrugged his shoulders. At the very same time, however, the Litvak decided to get to the bottom of this mystery.

That same evening, after final prayers, the Litvak sneaked into the rabbi's bedroom. He hid under the rabbi's bed and lay there. The Litvak had made up his mind to wait the whole night and see where the rabbi went and what he did during next morning's Slichoth prayers. Another person would probably have dozed off and dreamed the time away. But not the Litvak! He silently recited a whole section of the Holy Scriptures, either the one on vows or the one on sacrifices.

Before dawn the Litvak heard knocks on the door, calling people for Slichoth prayers. The rabbi had been awake for some time, moaning and tossing in his bed. His plaintive moans for the sorrows of his people could melt a soul. But not the Litvak's iron soul! The Litvak listened and lay low. The rabbi also stayed put. The rabbi, blessed be he, was on top of the bed and the Litvak under it.

After a while the Litvak heard beds creaking in other parts of the house. He heard people jumping out of their

34

beds, murmurings in Yiddish, water being poured, doors opening and closing. The house became dark and still when everyone, except the rabbi and the Litvak, had gone. Only a little light from the moon shone through the window shutters.

The Litvak was overcome by great fear when he was left all alone with the rabbi. His skin became taut with fright and the roots of his sideburns pricked his temples like needles. After all, was it a small matter to be left alone with the Rabbi of Nemirov, especially during the predawn time of Slichoth prayers? But the Litvak was stubborn and persisted.

At last the rabbi got up. First he said his daily prayers. Then he went over to his closet and took out a bundle. In the bundle were peasant clothes: linen pants, big boots, a coat, a large fur cap and a wide, long leather belt encrusted with brass nails. The rabbi put on these clothes. The end of a heavy rope stuck out from his pocket. The rabbi then left his bedchamber. The Litvak went after him. On the way out, the rabbi stopped in the kitchen. He took an ax from under a bench, put it under his belt and left the house.

The Litvak trembled, but he would not give up.

Silence hung over the darkened streets. Occasionally a wail of Slichoth prayers was heard from the synagogue, or the cry of a sick person escaped through a window. The rabbi kept to the sides of the streets, in the shadows of houses. He floated from one house to another; the Litvak followed him quietly.

The Litvak heard the beating of his heart merging with

the beats of the rabbi's steps. But he kept on walking behind the rabbi until they both reached the outskirts of
town.

Beyond the town was a small forest. The rabbi went into
the forest. He took thirty or maybe forty steps and halted
by a little tree. The Litvak was stunned to see the rabbi
take the ax from under his belt and begin to chop down the
tree. He kept on chopping until the tree groaned and snapped. When it fell, the rabbi cut it into logs, then the logs
into small sticks of wood. The rabbi made a bundle of the
wood and tied it with the rope from his pocket. He slung
the bundle over his shoulder, replaced the ax under his
belt, left the forest and walked back to town. The Litvak
followed a few paces behind.

The Rabbi of Nemirov stopped in a back alley before a
half-broken hut and knocked on the window.

"Who is it?" a frightened voice asked. The Litvak recognized the voice of an old, sick Jewish woman.

"Me," answered the rabbi in a coarse peasant accent.

"Who is 'me'?" asked the woman again.

The rabbi answered once more in the coarse tone of a
Russian peasant:

"Vassili!"

"Vassili who, and what do you want, Vassili?"

"Wood," answered the disguised Rabbi of Nemirov. "I
have wood for sale, very cheap, for next to nothing."
Without waiting for an answer the rabbi went into the
house.

The Litvak stole in behind him. By the gray light of
morning he saw a poor, ragged home, with broken fur-

nishings. A sick woman, covered with rags, lay in bed. In a bitter voice she asked:

"To buy? With what shall I buy? Where do I, a poor widow, have the money to buy?"

"I will lend it to you," answered the disguised rabbi. "It is only six cents."

"And how will I repay you?" groaned the woman.

"Foolish creature," reproached the rabbi. "Look, here you are, a poor sick woman, and I trust you with this small bundle of wood. I have faith that you will pay me for it. Yet you, who have such a great and mighty God, you do not trust in Him. You do not even trust in Him for a mere six cents of wood!"

"And who will light the fire for me?" lamented the widow. "Do I have the strength to get up?"

"I will also light the fire for you," said the rabbi.

As the rabbi was putting wood in the stove, he groaned and recited the first section of the Slichoth prayers. And when he lit the fire and the wood was burning merrily, he said in a cheerier tone the second part of the Slichoth prayers. The third section of the prayers he said as the fire burned fully and he was placing the covers back on the stove.

The Litvak observed all this silently, and thenceforth became a disciple of the Rabbi of Nemirov.

Later, when other members of his flock would relate that the Rabbi of Nemirov rose every morning during Slichoth prayers and flew to Heaven, the Litvak did not laugh, but would add quietly:

"If not still higher!"

# THE FAST

On a winter's night, Sarah sits by an oil lamp, darning socks. She works slowly, for her fingers are nearly frozen. Her lips are blue. She often puts down her work and runs around the room to warm her feet.

Four children are asleep on a bare straw mattress on one bed—two heads at each end, covered in the middle with old clothes. Now and then a child wakes and cries:

"I'm hungry!"

"Wait, children, wait," Sarah comforts. "Soon your father will return and bring you supper. I will wake you when he comes."

"Will we get something hot to eat?" the crying children ask. "We've had nothing hot to eat for days."

"Oh yes, something hot!" Sarah promises.

She does not believe the words she says. She looks around the room to see if there is anything left to pawn. There is nothing. Four bare, damp walls. A cracked stove. A few broken pots on the chimney piece. An old, bent, tin Chanukah lamp on the stove. The ceiling has a nail where a chandelier once might have hung. Two beds without bedding. Nothing more.

Sarah looks with pity at her sleeping children. Suddenly she turns her eyes toward the door. There are heavy steps on the staircase leading to the basement and the sound of cans clattering. A gleam of hope lights up her face.

She rubs one foot against the other for warmth, gets up with effort and opens the door. A pale, stooped man walks in.

"Well, Mendel?" Sarah asks softly.

The man puts down two empty cans, takes off the yoke from which they had hung, sighs and answers even more softly:

"Nothing, nothing. I wasn't paid. Everyone said, 'Tomorrow, the day after, at the beginning of the month!' "

"The children had nothing to eat all day," says Sarah. "Now, at last, they are asleep. Oh, my poor, poor children."

She cannot control herself and sobs.

"Why are you crying?" her husband asks.

"Oh, Mendel, the children are hungry! What's to become of us? It gets worse each day!"

"Worse? No, Sarah, not worse! It is a sin for you to say that. It was much worse last year! Not only did we not have bread, but we were also homeless. The children

40

roamed the streets all day, and slept in open courtyards at night. Now, at least, they have straw to sleep on and a roof over their heads."

Sarah sobs harder. She recalls their child who had died last year. He caught cold, grew hoarse and died. There had been no money for the doctor. No prayer for his recovery had been offered in the synagogue. The child had gone out like a candle.

"Don't cry, Sarah, please don't cry. Do not sin against God!" Mendel tries to comfort her.

"Oh, will God ever have pity on us?"

"Have pity on yourself! Do not take everything so to heart. Look at yourself. Our wedding day was only ten years ago. Then you were the prettiest girl in town! Look at your face now!"

"And you, Mendel? Remember when you were called Mendel the Mighty? Today you are stooped and sick, although you try to keep this secret from me. Oh my God, my God!" Sarah's cries wake the children.

"We want bread!"

"No! No one eats today!" says Mendel sternly.

The children sit up in alarm.

"Today is a fast day," continues Mendel grimly.

It takes a few minutes for the children to understand his words.

"What kind of fast? Tell us! What kind?" they cry tearfully.

Mendel says, with downcast eyes:

"The Holy Book, the Torah, fell off the pulpit in the synagogue during morning prayers. Therefore a fast was called to start at sundown. Even little babies must observe it."

The four children quiet down. Mendel continues:

"This is a fast like Yom Kippur, from sundown tonight until sundown tomorrow."

The children tumble out of bed and dance barefoot around the room.

"We will fast, fast, fast!"

Mendel screens the light of the oil lamp with his shoulders. He does not want his children to see their mother's tears.

"Well, that will be enough!" He tries to calm the children. "Dancing is not allowed during a fast! You will dance during the holiday of Simchath Torah, when we rejoice in the Law!"

The children go back to bed. Their hunger is forgotten. One little girl begins to sing "Our Father," "On the High Mountain" and other hymns. A cold shiver runs down Mendel's spine.

"Singing also is forbidden," he whispers. The children quiet down and, worn out from singing and dancing, fall asleep. Only Chaiml, the oldest boy, is not fully asleep and asks:

"Papa, when will I be bar mitzvah?"

"It's still a long time off, Chaiml. In four more years you will be thirteen."

"Will you buy me phylacteries?"

"Of course."

"And a little prayerbook with gilt edges?"

"Yes, with God's help, I will."

"Then will I fast on *all* fast days?"
"Yes, Chaiml, on all fast days."
Quietly Mendel adds:
"Lord of the Universe, but not on fast days like today."

# THE MATCH

This lovely story is true. It happened long, long ago in the land of Moravia, where Jews did not live near one another in large cities or towns. They lived in scattered villages and forests, isolated from one another, without the Torah and without community prayers. Only for Rosh Hashanah did they gather their families together and go to a synagogue in a far-away town.

A Jewish dairy farmer lived at that time on a nobleman's estate. This dairy farmer was rich. He milked five hundred cows for the nobleman and had cows of his own as well. His cellar was filled with cheese and butter; his attic was filled with corn, flax and furs. His wallet was stuffed with money. His wife had savings of her own as well. Their only son was a healthy, sturdy lad, growing tall like a young tree in the forest.

Yet one winter evening, as the farmer went over his account books by candlelight, he looked sad. From time to time he gazed out of the window with worried, tearful eyes.

"It is a sin to worry so much, dear husband!" His wife's words roused him from his deep thoughts. She had just come in from the next room where their son was sleeping.

"Our son looks well." She beamed. "His cheeks are as rosy as the morning. His breath is peaceful and steady, and smells of fresh apples."

"The future of our son is on my mind," answered the dairy farmer. "We live in an isolated settlement, far away from other Jews. The years fly by. How shall we find a proper wife for our son? Will he ever marry?"

"God will help us. He hasn't forsaken us so far," said his wife consolingly.

"Yes, yes, you are right. We do need God's help, but why should He help us? I'm no scholar. I don't study the Torah, and we don't live among Jews," answered the farmer. "We can perform only one good deed, the giving of hospitality to strangers. But how can we do that now? Look!" He pointed at the window.

A heavy snow was falling, covering roads and blocking paths. It might be weeks or even months before anyone could reach their threshold. The farmer got up and went outside to check the roads. His wife began to make beds for the night. The farmer lingered outside and his wife became uneasy. She put down the bedding and went over to the window, hoping to attract her husband's attention. She tapped on the windowpane with her stubby fingers, but the pane was covered with ice and made no sound. So she put a shawl around her shoulders and went outside, too.

The farmer did not hear his wife and did not turn around. He seemed in a trance as he looked at the road leading from the woods. His wife looked questioningly in the same direction. An old woman was coming toward them. She wore a high bonnet and was covered only with a light paisley shawl, as if she were strolling on a fine summer night. The shawl could not protect her from the bitter cold. Its ends flew left and right, like wings. The woman did not walk on the snow—she floated above it.

The farmer and his wife gaped. When the woman came near them, she asked whether she could rest for an hour in their house. The couple smiled at each other and led their visitor joyfully into their house.

The farmer's wife rushed over to the cupboard and took out all manner of good things to eat and drink—cakes and biscuits, jam and sweet brandy. But the guest said that she was not hungry; she merely wished to rest. The farmer's wife lit a wax candle and took the guest to a separate room. She fixed for her a comfortable bed, with snow-white linen, soft goose-down pillows and a warm woolen blanket.

"If you do not wish to eat or drink, then sleep in good health."

"I do not wish to sleep," the woman said. "I only wish to rest awhile, for I have far to go."

As the farmer's wife was about to leave, the woman asked what she owed them for the room.

"I want to leave quietly and not disturb or wake anyone. I would like to pay you now."

The farmer's wife was deeply hurt.

"I will not accept money! No, no, I will not take money! The only good deed we can perform in our isolated home is giving hospitality to strangers. God looks after us because of this, and I hope that He will help us also in the future."

The guest smiled and said:

"Is there anything you need? Do you have any requests of Heaven?"

"God forbid," the farmer's wife replied. "My husband and I are in good health. Our son is well, too. We have more money than we need. The only thing we want is a good and proper bride for our son. He is almost seventeen years old, and we live in this isolated settlement, far from any Jewish community. How will we ever find a proper wife for our boy?"

"What are you doing about it?" asked the guest.

"We trust in God. We pray to him. My husband prays in his own way. I pray in mine. I say all the prayers which Sarah Bath Tuvim wrote long, long ago. I know them all by heart. I often cry over her special prayers for a proper marriage for a son."

"God will help you," said the guest with a sweet smile.

"I am sure of that. Since you will not let me pay you for the room, I will give you a present for your son's future bride."

The woman took out from under her paisley shawl a pair of dazzling golden slippers, embroidered with pearls, and gave them to the farmer's wife.

"A gift from Sarah Bath Tuvim," she said, and then she vanished.

The farmer, worried that his wife had been gone so long, knocked on the guest-room door. When he received no answer, he opened the door. In the middle of the room stood his wife, her eyes bulging and her mouth open, with a pair of dazzling golden slippers in her hands.

At the same time, also in Moravia, but miles and miles away from the farmer's home, lived a Jewish charcoal maker. His home was in a deep forest, where he leased a little hut and oven from the nobleman who owned the land. This Jew was very poor, and his work was hard. Winter and summer he gathered dead bark and branches felled by storms. He carried these to his oven and made charcoal.

He was a widower, but the Lord had blessed him with a good daughter. When he came home at night, blackened and tired from his work, she greeted him joyfully. She helped him wash and laid out fresh clothes for him. She cooked his meals and made his bed.

Sometimes when the charcoal maker could not sleep, his daughter lit a stick of wood and read to him her Yiddish translations of the Holy Books. She also read the special prayers of Sarah Bath Tuvim, until he fell asleep, lulled by her sweet voice and the holy words.

One night she read aloud a mother's prayers for a good husband for her child.

"Dear God, see about a bridegroom for my dear and loving daughter. Find for her a proper Jewish husband . . ."

When the girl realized what she had read, she became embarrassed and stopped.

"Do not stop, dear daughter. Please go on. Let us pray to God for you together. I have a loving heart, my child, but I am a simple Jew, without learning. I do not know the words of prayer."

She obeyed and read on. The prayers wafted around the room like sweet perfume. Her father fell asleep, but she did not notice. He snored and she did not hear. She read on and on and on. An unfamiliar longing wakened in her heart. Her voice trembled. Her eyes filled with tears.

Suddenly the door opened and a strange woman came in. She wore a high bonnet and was covered with a paisley shawl. The woman's eyes shone brightly and her wizened old face beamed.

"Papa!" The frightened girl tried to wake her father. The old woman put a finger to her lips, then drew the girl close to her.

"Do not be afraid, my child. I am Sarah Bath Tuvim. Since it is a quiet night, I heard your prayers. I came here to give you a gift." She took out the gift from under her paisley shawl.

"Here is silk velvet, just the right size for a bag. Here

are pearls, silk floss, fringes, and silver and gold thread, too. I will show you how to sew this bag, and how to embroider it as well. Here you will make the Star of David, and there you will embroider little flowers. This will be a bag for your future bridegroom's phylacteries, just like the one your mother made for your father."

The young girl sewed and embroidered all night, doing everything Sarah Bath Tuvim told her. When dawn came and the charcoal maker woke up, Sarah Bath Tuvim was gone, but his daughter held in her lap a beautiful bag made of velvet, silver, gold and pearls.

When the farmer's son became seventeen years old, his parents sent him out into the world to look for a proper bride. Her feet would have to fit Sarah Bath Tuvim's slippers.

The young man traveled, by horse and cart, through forests, settlements, villages and towns. Girls were as plentiful as earth and sand, but not one girl's feet would fit the slippers. The young man traveled one year, and then he traveled two years, but he did not find the proper girl. He lost all interest and decided to go back home. He would tell his parents that the whole thing was a dream, that such tiny feet did not exist.

On his way back home, the young man got lost in a dense forest. Hundreds of oaks stood like giants, blocking paths, barring roads. The sun was sinking on the horizon like a giant fireball. He stopped, for it was Friday afternoon, and traveling was forbidden after sundown before the Sabbath.

When evening set in, he began to chant the Song of Songs. The trees whispered quietly in the evening breeze, as if they too were chanting. The woods became ever quieter and darker. Suddenly a light flickered between the trees. The young man ran joyfully toward the light, and saw a little hut. He knocked on the window.

"Does a Jew live here?"

"Yes, a Jew."

A man came out of the hut.

"Peace be with you."

"Peace to you," answered the young man. "May I observe the Sabbath with you?"

"You may," answered the man with a sad smile, "but I am a poor charcoal maker and have no proper Sabbath meal to share with you."

"I have enough food, and wine as well, in my wagon," answered the young man. "We will get it and bring it to your house."

After chanting Sabbath prayers and singing hymns, the charcoal maker and the young man sat down to a fine supper. While they ate, the young man noticed that the old man took only one bite of each delicacy. The rest of the food he carried to the door.

The young man wondered. Perhaps the old man gave his food to a calf or horse? If he had animals, he could not be poor! And if he was not poor, why did he not prepare a proper meal for welcoming the Sabbath? Being young, and not at all timid, the young man asked the charcoal maker.

"No, young man, I do not have a calf or horse. I do have a sweet daughter, but she has no shoes, poor thing. She is embarrassed to come in barefoot, so she eats outside. . . ."

The young man's heart beat wildly. He quickly took out the golden slippers from his pocket and gave them to the charcoal maker.

"Go and ask your daughter to try these on. Maybe they will fit!"

The charcoal maker returned. "They fit!" he said simply.

A marriage was arranged between the rich dairy farmer's son and the poor charcoal maker's daughter. The wedding was held at the home of the dairy farmer. When the bridal party stepped away from the wedding canopy, a woman in a high bonnet and a paisley shawl appeared. As she moved lightly toward bride and groom, her wizened face beamed.

Not everyone knew who this woman was!

# MIRACLES ON THE SEA

In the land of Holland, a Jewish fisherman named Satye lived in a half-sunken hut on the edge of the sea. A descendant of generations of fishermen, he had spent days, months and years by the sea. Satye caught fish, his wife mended nets and kept house. Their children played in the sand.

Perhaps Satye was named after his great-grandfather Saadie, but of that he knew very little. In fact, he knew very little of his ancestry and of his Jewishness. His was the only Jewish family in the fishing village. How much could he have known of his Jewishness?

When Satye went to sea with other fishermen and storms endangered his life, neither he nor his family could cry out even the "Shema Israel" prayer: "Hear, O Israel!

55

The Lord is our God, the Lord is One." Satye would look silently at the sky, his wife would clutch her head and throw angry looks toward Heaven. His children would throw themselves onto the sand and cry out, with other children of the village: "Sancta Maria! Sancta Maria!"

How should they have known better? Their home was much too far away for the family to make regular visits to a Jewish community. They barely eked out a living, and could not afford to ride. Besides, the sea did not allow them to get away. Satye's father, grandfather and great-grandfather had perished on the sea. And though Satye knew that the sea was his worst enemy, he loved it and could not tear himself away from it. He wanted to live by the sea and to die by the sea.

However, Satye and his family retained one Jewish custom. They always observed Yom Kippur, the day for fasting and atonement. Each year, early in the morning on the day before Yom Kippur, Satye and his family chose the biggest fish from their catch. Then they walked to town. Once in town, they gave the fish to the Jewish community's shochet, the kosher butcher, with whom they ate before and after the fast.

During the holy day of Yom Kippur, the whole family sat in the synagogue. They listened to the choir and the playing of the organ, and to the singing and the chanting of the cantor. They did not understand a single word of the service. Satye and his family looked at the Holy Ark that held the Torahs, and at the rabbi in his golden skullcap. When the golden skullcap got up, they got up; when the golden skullcap sat down, they sat down. Sometimes, when Satye napped out of weariness, his neighbor poked him with his elbow.

All Satye knew about Yom Kippur was that he could not work, neither fish nor row, that he had to fast from sundown to sundown, and that he had to listen to the choir and the organ and the cantor in the synagogue. He did not know that even fish of the sea trembled on this day, that momentous things went on in Heaven.

Satye knew that after the final prayer of Yom Kippur, the Neilah, he would go to supper with the butcher. Perhaps even the butcher did not know more.

After supper and coffee, Satye and his family would say goodbye to the butcher and his family. They would wish each other good fortune for the year ahead. Then Satye and his family would leave and walk all night toward the sea. They did not say "home," but "to the sea!" It was impossible to keep them in town.

Sometimes the butcher and his wife chided Satye:

"You did not even see the town!"

"Hm, the town!" Satye would grimace. Satye did not talk much. The sea had taught him silence. But he did speak of his hatred for the town:

"It is crowded! Only a ribbon of sky between roofs! There is space by the sea, you can breathe by the sea!"

"But the sea is your enemy, your death," the butcher argued.

"But a good death it is!" Satye answered.

He wished for the same end that his father and grandfather and great-grandfather had had. To be swallowed healthy by the sea, not to be sick and stay in bed, and then be buried in the hard earth.

Brr! A chill would go through Satye when he thought of such a death. And so each year after Yom Kippur the family walked happily back to the sea—home to the sea.

Years went by. Fishermen came and went; the butchers also changed. But the Yom Kippur custom always remained the same. Satye fasted, listened to the choir, cantor and organ, wished the butcher a good year and went home.

This was the only thread that held Satye to his Jewishness and his people.

It came to pass one morning that the eastern horizon was turning red and the sea was waking silently. Here and there a few birds fluttered against the blue sky. Beams of light floated above the sea. Golden rays slid over the yellow sand.

It was the morning before Yom Kippur. All the fishing huts were closed. Only one door creaked. Satye came out. His face was earnest, but his eyes sparkled. He was off to catch a fish for Yom Kippur. He untied the chains that moored his little boat. The chain rattled. At once voices were heard from all directions. Satye's neighbors were calling to him:

"Don't go, Satye, don't go!"

The wide sea lay peaceful and quiet, barely breathing,

hardly audible. Smiles seemed to dance between its ripples, as on the wrinkled face of a kind old grandmother. But the fishermen knew the sea well. Today they did not trust it.

"Don't go, Satye, don't go!"

An old man with fluttering gray hair and a wrinkled face came out of his house. He went over to Satye and put his hand on Satye's shoulder.

"Look!"

The old man pointed to a little dot on the horizon, a tiny dot that only a fisherman's eyes could see.

"A cloud will grow from that dot! The sea will rock; its sparkling surface will break. The sea's playfulness will become grim; the ripples will become huge waves that will swallow big and little boats as Leviathan swallows fish."

"I'll be home before it happens," Satye said. "I only have to catch one fish."

The face of the old man grew serious.

"You have a wife and children, Satye!"

"And God in Heaven, too!" answered Satye confidently. He pushed his little boat off shore and jumped in. Light as a feather the boat glided out to sea. The sea caressed it sweetly, lovingly. The old fisherman murmured on shore: "Sancta Maria, Sancta Maria."

Satye's boat moved swiftly over the sea. Skilfully he threw his nets into the water. They became heavy, and Satye pulled them up with all his might. In his nets he found all kinds of weeds, but no fish. Again and again he threw down the nets and pulled them up, to find only weeds.

The sea began to rock. The sun was still in the sky, but its radiance was becoming misty. A crying sun. Like a brown snake the little dot on the horizon sidled up to the sun. Nearly half the day was gone, and Satye had not caught a fish.

"God must not want me to catch a fish this year. He does not want me to perform my good deed for Yom Kippur."

Satye decided to return home and turned his little boat toward shore. At that instant his face was splashed with water. A big golden fish was cavorting on the waves, splashing water with its shiny fins.

"Oh, I must catch *this* fish!" said Satye. He decided that God, after all, willed him to have a fish. He turned his boat back out to sea and gave chase to the golden fish.

The sea foamed and waves rose ever higher. The sun was almost completely hidden. The golden fish swam on the crests of waves, and Satye's boat pursued it swiftly. As suddenly as it had come, the golden fish disappeared from view. An enormous, sky-high wave rose between the fish and Satye's boat.

"This fish is playing tricks on me!"

Satye turned his boat again to shore, and at that very moment the wave subsided. The golden fish appeared near the boat and looked at Satye, as if pleading:

"Take me, take me!"

Again Satye chased the fish. Again the fish disappeared. The furious sea came between the fish and Satye. As if afraid, the sun hid behind the clouds. The wind seemed to have waited for the disappearance of the sun. Now it lashed out with immense power. The sea thundered as if thousands of bass viols were playing in its depths and pounded as if thousands of drums were beating in its waves.

"I must go home!" Satye's heart was beating wildly. He pulled his nets into the boat and grasped the oars with all his might. The veins in his hands seemed about to burst.

Like an empty nutshell the little boat was thrown about by the waves. As Satye rowed toward shore, the sky went black and the sea turned an angry brown.

Suddenly Satye saw a woman swimming toward him. Her floating hair was black, like his wife's hair. Beneath her hair he saw white hands. His wife had such hands. A voice called out: "Help!" It was the voice of his wife, the mother of his children. She must have followed him in their second boat. Now she was drowning, calling for his help. He turned the boat to reach his wife, but the sea would not allow it. Waves rose, the storm screamed and howled. In all this noise Satye still heard the woman's voice: "Help, Satye, help!"

With his last ounce of strength Satye rowed to her, but when he was near the spot, he could not see her any more. A huge wave rose and hurled the boat one way and the woman another.

"A mirage!" Satye remembered that the same thing had happened to him with the golden fish. Suddenly he turned his gaze toward shore and realized that it was sundown.

61

The lights were lit in all the fishermen's houses.

"Yom Kippur has begun!" He let the oars drop from his hands. "Do with me as You wish," he cried toward Heaven, "but on Yom Kippur I will not row."

The wind raged on. Enormous waves pummeled the boat. Satye sat peacefully in his boat and looked up toward Heaven. Suddenly he remembered a melody the temple choir had sung, and he began to hum. The sky got ever darker, the wind blew ever more sharply. A wave tore an oar from Satye's hand and threw it away. Another wave chased the little boat as if with open jaws. In the midst of all this uproar Satye sang a melody. Perhaps Satye's silent soul could only speak to God through song?

His boat turned over. Satye wanted to die singing, but he was not destined to die yet. Two figures, with flowing hair and glowing eyes, came out of the mist and walked over the waves toward Satye. They picked him up, placed him between them and walked with him over the waves, as if over hills and dales. They led him, arm-in-arm, through wind and tumult. He tried to speak, but they would not let him.

"Sing, Satye, sing! Your song will overcome the anger of the sea."

Walking over waves toward the shore, Satye heard his little boat following them. He turned around and saw his nets all tangled up in the boat. The golden fish was in his nets. The two figures put Satye down on shore and disappeared.

In his house, Satye met the butcher and the butcher's

wife talking to his wife and children. There had been a fire
in town, so they had come to visit Satye and his family.

They ate the fish and celebrated Yom Kippur together,
as always.

# BONTCHE THE SILENT

Here, in this world, the death of Bontche made no impression on anyone at all. No one knew who Bontche was, how he lived, of what he died. No one cared whether his heart had burst, or his strength had given out, or whether he had simply died of hunger.

Bontche lived quietly and he died quietly. He went through our world like a shadow. At Bontche's birth there had been no drinking of wine. At his bar mitzvah he had not made a fiery speech. He lived like a little grain of sand by the edge of the sea, among millions just like him. When the wind picked him up and blew him to the other side of the sea, no one even noticed.

After Bontche died and was buried, the wind blew off his grave the little wooden plaque on which his name was written. The gravedigger's wife found it far away from Bontche's grave. She used it as fuel for cooking potatoes. Three days after Bontche's death not even the gravedigger knew where he had buried him.

Bontche's likeness did not remain in anyone's mind or heart. No trace or memory of him remained. He lived alone and he died alone.

But for the noise and commotion created by people in this world, perhaps someone would have heard Bontche's backbone crack under his heavy loads. Even when he did not have a load on his back, his head drooped toward earth—as if he were looking for his grave while still alive. If the world had had more time, perhaps someone would have asked:

"Whatever became of Bontche?"

But it was not so in the Next World. There Bontche's death was known to all. The Messianic horn resounded in all the seven heavens. In Paradise there was a joyous tumult:

"Bontche the Silent is dead! Bontche has left the earth!"

Young angels with sparkling eyes, gold filigree wings and silver slippers ran around joyfully and told each other:

"Bontche the Silent is coming! Just imagine!"

The rustle of their wings, the tapping of their slippers and their happy laughter filled the heavens and even reached the Almighty's throne. God Himself knew that Bontche the Silent was on the way.

The angels caught Bontche in midair and played a hymn

for him. Father Abraham shook hands with him as if he were an old, dear friend.

When Bontche was told that a throne was ready for him in Heaven, that a crown was waiting for his head, that not one word would be wasted on his case before the Heavenly Court—Bontche, just as in the other world, kept silent from fear. He was sure that it was all a dream, or simply a mistake.

He was used to that. Many times in his lifetime he had dreamed that he was gathering gold off the ground, and then awakened poorer than ever.

"My luck was like that," Bontche thought. He was afraid to let a sound escape his lips, to move a muscle, lest he be recognized and thrown into hell.

Bontche shivered. He did not hear the angels' compliments, did not see them dancing around him. He did not answer Father Abraham's "Peace be with you" greeting. When he was led into the chambers of the Heavenly Court, he did not say, "Good morning."

Bontche was scared out of his senses. His fear multiplied when he noticed the floor of the Heavenly Court's chamber—pure alabaster, set with diamonds.

"Am I standing on this floor?" Bontche was nearly paralyzed. "Who knows what hero, rabbi, saint they have in mind? He will come, and that will be my end."

He did not even see the President of the Court hand over papers to the Defending Angel, nor hear his admonishment:

"Read these, but be brief."

The great chamber seemed to swirl around poor Bontche's head. His ears buzzed. At last the Defending Angel's sweet voice was heard:

"His name fitted him like a suit made by a master tailor for a slender figure."

"What's he saying?" Bontche wondered. Immediately the President's impatient voice interrupted:

"No similes, please!"

The Defending Angel started again.

"He never complained about anybody, neither God nor man. Hate never burned in his heart. He never raised his eyes with a complaint to Heaven."

Bontche still did not understand a word. The harsh voice of the President of the Court interrupted again:

"No rhetoric, please!"

"Job gave in, yet Bontche was even more unfortunate than he!"

"I want facts, only facts!" the President called out impatiently.

"He was silent when his mother died and when, at thirteen, he got a stepmother who was a snake, a real viper."

"Perhaps they really do mean me?" Bontche wondered.

"Without insinuations against third parties!" snapped the President of the Court.

"She begrudged him every bite of food. She gave him moldy bread while she herself drank sweet coffee with cream."

"Speak to the point!" commanded the President of the Court.

"She beat Bontche till he was black and blue. He wore torn and musty clothes. In wintertime, barefoot, he chopped wood for her in the courtyard. His hands were weak and young, the logs were thick, the hatchet blunt. Many times he wrenched his wrist! Many times his feet became frostbitten. But he kept silent, even to his own father . . ."

The Prosecuting Angel laughed.

"To that drunkard?"

Bontche felt cold in every limb.

". . . he did not complain."

The Defending Angel continued.

"He was always alone. He had no friends, no learning, no new clothes, not even a free minute to himself."

"Facts!" called out the President of the Court again. The Defending Angel went on:

"Bontche was silent later, when in a drunken rage his father threw him out of the house. He got up quickly from the snow and ran away. Even when he was hungry, he begged only with his eyes.

"One stormy night he came to a big town. He walked into this town as a drop of water falls into the ocean. Yet he spent his first night there under arrest. He was silent, he did not ask, 'Why? For what?' When he was released, he looked for work. It was hard for him to find a job, yet he did not complain.

"When he did find work, he never counted how many pounds of burden he had to carry to earn a penny. He never counted the times he fell while working for practically nothing. He never thought about the difference between his lot and that of others—he was always silent.

"He did not demand his wages loudly. Like a beggar, he

would stand and wait. 'Come later,' he was often told. Silently, ghostlike, he would disappear.

"He was even silent when he was cheated out of his earnings, or when a counterfeit coin was given to him."

"They must mean me!" Bontche felt reassured.

"Once," continued the Defending Angel, "a change came into his life. A carriage with wild horses came flying down the road. The driver of the carriage lay on the pavement with a cracked skull. The horses foamed at their mouths, sparks came from their hoofs and their eyes burned like torches on a dark night. In the carriage sat a man, half alive, half dead from fright. And Bontche stopped the horses! The man he saved was a charitable Jew. He handed the dead driver's whip to Bontche and made him a coachman. What's more, the charitable Jew found for him a wife!"

"They do mean me, me, me!" rejoiced Bontche, yet did not dare to raise his eyes to the Heavenly Court.

The Defending Angel went on speaking:

"Bontche was silent when his benefactor later went bankrupt and did not pay his wages. He was silent when his wife ran away and left him with their little baby. He was silent when his child grew up and threw him out of his own house."

"They must mean me!" Bontche thought.

"He was silent even when his benefactor paid off all his debts except those to Bontche," continued the Defending Angel sadly. "Bontche was silent when the man, again riding in a carriage with wild horses, ran over

Bontche and wounded him. He did not tell the police the name of the man who ran over him.

"Even in the hospital, where most people cry, Bontche was silent. He was silent even when the doctor refused to go near his bed unless he was paid beforehand, or when the hospital attendant did not change his sheets unless he got his five cents. He was silent when death came. Not a word against God, not a word against men!

"I have spoken!" The Defending Angel finished.

Bontche trembled. He knew that after the Defending Angel came the Prosecuting Angel. Who knew what he would say? Bontche himself did not remember his life. Here in Heaven he had forgotten what had happened to him in the previous world. The Defending Angel had reminded him of almost everything. Who knew what the Prosecuting Angel might remind him of?

"Gentlemen!" The Prosecuting Angel's sharp voice begins, and stops.

"Gentlemen!" he begins again more softly, and stops once more.

Almost gently the Prosecuting Angel then says:

"Gentlemen, as Bontche was always silent, so shall I be silent!"

There is utter silence in the chamber of the Heavenly Court. Then a tremulous new voice is heard:

"Bontche! My child Bontche!" The voice sounds like the music of a harp. "My dear child Bontche!"

Bontche's soul weeps. He wants to lift his eyes, but

71

they are filled with tears. Bontche has never felt such sweet emotion.

"My child, my Bontche!" Bontche has not heard such words since his mother died.

"My child, you have suffered so much," says the President of the Court kindly. "There was no limb, no bone in your body that had no wounds. There was no spot on your soul that had not bled. Yet you were always silent. In the other world they did not understand you. Perhaps you yourself did not know that you could have cried out, and that your cries would have been heard. You did not know of your own power.

"On earth your silence was not rewarded. That was the world of lies. Here, in the World of Truth, you will receive your reward. The Heavenly Court will not judge you. It will not sentence you. It will not mete out a reward. Take whatever you want. *Everything* here is yours!"

Bontche raises his eyes for the first time. He is almost blinded by the heavenly lights. Everything around him sparkles, dazzles, shines—the walls, the vessels, the angels, everything!

"Really?" he asks uncertainly and shyly.

"Of course!" the President of the Court assures him. "Everything here is yours, everything in Heaven belongs to you. Choose whatever you wish; you will only take what is already yours."

"Really?" asks Bontche again, but this time with more confidence.

"Really, really, really!" he is told from all directions.

"Well, if that be so"—Bontche smiles—"then I would like a hot roll with fresh butter every morning."

The Defending Angel, the President of the Court and all the angels lower their heads in sadness and shame. The Prosecuting Angel laughs.

# THE CASE AGAINST
# THE WIND

The poor widow Shunamith lived long, long ago, in the days of King Solomon. She lived in a small hut in a fishing village on the edge of the Mediterranean Sea. She made her living by the toil of her own hands, making and fixing nets for fishermen.

Once, a time of great winds and storms came to her village. No boats went out to sea, and no nets were spread. Shunamith could not make a living. She was left entirely without bread. She could not go into the poor fishermen's homes to ask for any, for none of them had bread, either. So Shunamith decided to seek bread elsewhere.

A very rich and pious Jew lived a few miles away from her fishing village. God blessed this man with fertile fields, fruit-laden orchards and huge forests of olive trees. He had herds of sheep and cattle, mules and camels. His large house was built in a huge yard.

One morning, when Shunamith got up, she saw that the sky was still angry and the air was still windy. She decided to go to see the rich Jew. Over her shoulders she put an old shawl, which she wore during the day and with which she covered herself at night, and left her village. Toward midday she reached the rich man's yard. She met him by his door. She bowed before him, and with her forehead touched the ground three times near his feet.

"Why do you bow to me, woman? Get up and tell me your name and what you want of me," he said.

"I am the widow Shunamith, and I came from the fishing village by the sea. It is long since I have had anything to eat. I came to ask you for a piece of bread."

"Listen, woman," the man replied. "I have just returned from Jerusalem, where I saw King Solomon's castle. A glorious sight! Everyone was permitted to enter the palace, and so I too went in. King Solomon sat on a golden throne, surrounded by servants and advisers, and by common folk, too. King Solomon was reading to the people from the Holy Books. Listen carefully to what he said:

" 'He who abhors gifts will live long. He who accepts things for nothing shortens his own God-given life.'

"You wish to sin, woman," the rich man continued, "and I cannot be a partner to your sin. God remembers everything. He will not forget that I have helped you to shorten your own life. I cannot give you anything for free."

"If that is so," said the widow, "do not give me any-thing for free. Lend me a loaf of bread, or lend me some flour so I can take it home and bake bread. It will save my life. I will thank you and pray for you to the Almighty."

"This I cannot do either," answered the rich and pious man. "King Solomon also said: 'Whoever lends, en-slaves!' If ever I had slaves, they would be strangers, not descendants of Abraham. I do not wish to enslave my own flesh and blood, and especially not a widow. I cannot lend you anything and I cannot permit you to be in debt to me."

"Shall I collapse from hunger by your feet?" the widow asked. "Will that please God, the protector of orphans and widows, any better?"

"Widow Shunamith, you will not collapse from hunger by my feet," he answered her gently. "I will help you, as God is my witness, but I will help you with advice. Go and take advantage of ownerless property, property which be-longs to no one."

"What do you mean by that? Ownerless property can only be found in the wilderness, in the desert! It would take me three days to get there, and what would I find? Dried-out grass? Are you making fun of a poor widow? Are you not afraid of Him who always watches out for poor widows and orphans?"

"I am not making fun of you," the man answered. "God-fearing I am from birth, and I do not send you into the wilderness to gather grass. Cock your ear, woman, and listen to me well! My warehouse is empty now. I carried one hundred sacks of snow-white flour to King Solomon's palace. The boards in my warehouse are covered with flour-dust which seeped through the sacks. This dust is ownerless, this dust is not mine. Go to my warehouse and sweep the boards. Collect the dust of the snow-white flour and take it home. Gather twigs along the way. When you get home, make a fire, bake bread and praise God."

Shunamith did what the rich and pious man had advised her to do. She swept and collected the flour dust from the rich man's warehouse, and on her way back home she gathered twigs. It was dark when she reached her hut. She made a fire, then mixed the flour with water. She made three small, flat rounds of bread which barely fit on her little fire.

As she was praising God and was about to eat the first flat bread, her door suddenly opened. A man rushed in, screaming:

"Save a man from death! It's been three days and nights since I have eaten!"

And he told Shunamith the following tale:

In the middle of the night a fire had broken out in his village. The fire seemed to come down from the sky. The wind blew it through his whole village. Everyone and everything—women, children, men and cattle—burned. He alone was saved from the flames. For three days now he had been running, pursued by fear and by the memory of the fire—and without a bite of bread to eat.

Shunamith handed her little, flat bread to the man and said:

"Go out, for I am alone in this hut. Eat and save yourself."

The man took the bread and disappeared into the dark night.

Shunamith thanked the Lord that He had given her bread, and that He had also given her a chance to perform a good deed. As she was about to take a bite of her second round of bread, the door opened again with great force. Another man rushed in, crying:

"Save a man from death!"

And he told this tale to Shunamith:

He had been a rich man and owned great herds of sheep and cattle. He had lived with his wife and children in richly appointed rooms and had many men to tend his herds. One day, as if on the wind's wings, Bedouins came with bows and arrows in their hands. They killed his wife and children and took away his herds. Then they disappeared into the desert. When the desert stopped reverberating from the sound of their horses, he got up and saw that he alone had been saved. For three days and nights now he had been wandering, without anything to eat.

"Give me bread, or I'll die right here!"

With kindness in her heart, Shunamith handed him her second little, flat bread. She praised God that He had given her another chance to perform a good deed.

"Eat the bread outside my door, for I am alone," she told the man. He took the bread and also disappeared into the darkness of the night.

As Shunamith was about to put the third round of bread into her mouth, an immense north wind tore into her little hut. It blew away the walls and roof. Then the wind tore the third flat bread out of Shunamith's hands and cast it into the sea.

Immediately after that the wind and rain stopped. The storm subsided. The sea became peaceful as the first rays of sun appeared over the water. Soon the fishermen would awake, untie the boats on shore and joyfully spread out their nets. The time of winds and storms was over! Children would run out of huts and play! Everyone would call out happily to each other:

"No more hunger, blessed be God!"

There would be bread!

But Shunamith did not rejoice. Her mind was full of angry thoughts.

"What did God want from me? One bread He took away to give to a man saved from a fire. That was right, blessed be His name. The second bread He took away for one saved from robbers, also blessed be His name. He gave and He took away for those needier than I.

"But the third bread? The wind just tore it out of a poor widow's hands and cast it into the sea! Why would the wind do such an evil thing? Perhaps God did not even know about it? Perhaps the wind did it of its own will, without God's knowledge and against His will? The wind did it just for spite! I know that it could not be otherwise!"

Shunamith decided that she would not forgive her torturer, the mean wind. She would report the wind! But to whom should she report the wind? Shunamith decided that she would go to Jerusalem and take up the case against the wind with King Solomon!

Hungry and exhausted, but driven by a righteous wrath, she walked the long road to Jerusalem. When she finally reached it, she was shown to the king's palace. King Solomon's doors were open to one and all, and especially to poor widows. The guards let her in. When Shunamith came into the Great Hall, she fell on her knees before King Solomon.

"My Lord," she said, "I have a case to bring before you."

"Against whom? I see that you have come alone."

"Against the wind," Shunamith answered. She raised her face to the king and told him of her complaint.

"Very well," King Solomon answered. "Your face is your best witness. It is tired. Hunger burns in your eyes. First of all, refresh yourself. Sit down in the corner and rest. Bread and wine will be served to you. Eat, drink and regain your strength. You will receive my verdict later."

Shunamith sat down in a corner of the Great Hall. Servants brought her bread and wine. As she ate, three men entered, carrying heavy sacks on their shoulders. The men wished to speak to King Solomon.

"What are your wishes, strangers? And what are you carrying in those sacks?" the king asked. The three men took turns in telling this tale to King Solomon:

"We are Arab traders, descendants of Ishmael. We trade in fine jewels, vessels and exotic spices. Recently we were traveling in our boat when great winds came to sea. But though the sea was very stormy, we were not afraid.

"One evening, however, our little boat began to leak. We found a hole in the boat, but we had nothing with which to plug it. We screamed and cried, hoping that someone on shore would hear us. But the wind captured our cries and ran away with them into the night. Our boat began to sink. We cried to our god, but he did not hear us. We cried to other gods—to the god of Moab, to the god of the Philistines, to other gods. None answered us. Somehow we recalled that there was still another god, the God of Israel. We cried out to Him: 'God of Israel, answer us in our time of need!' We made a vow that we would give to this God all of our silver and all of our gold, if He would only save us.

" 'Save us, rescue us, God of Israel!' we cried.

"At that very instant the wind became much stronger. With extraordinary force it flung something at our boat and plugged the leak. Then the wind subsided, and we reached the shore in peace.

"When we came ashore, we asked people where the God of Israel lived. They told us to go to Jerusalem. And so we came with our sacks of gold and silver to Jerusalem and we asked people:

" 'Where is your God? We want to see Him!'

"People answered us that the God of Israel cannot be seen. 'But we must thank Him, honor Him, and give Him offerings,' we said. People shrugged their shoulders. Some even laughed at us. Then a very old man advised us to turn to you, great sage and king. You are, he said, the wisest man in all the world, and you will tell us how to keep our vow. You will know how to dispose of our silver and our gold in a manner which will be pleasing to the God of Israel."

The three Arab traders finished their tale and bowed. King Solomon then asked them:

"Did you examine what the wind had blown in from shore to plug the leak in your boat?"

"We did," they answered. "When we reached shore we examined it carefully. We saw that it was a small, barely baked, flat round of bread. We brought it with us and can show it to you."

The oldest of the three traders took the bread out of his pocket and showed it to King Solomon.

King Solomon asked the widow Shunamith whether it was her little, flat bread. She recognized it—it was her bread.

King Solomon decreed there and then that the widow Shunamith would get all of the gold and silver which the Arab traders brought in their sacks. They gave the gold and silver to her, thanked the king and went away.

And King Solomon said to Shunamith:

"Take this gold and silver. God rewarded you for your third bread. You must realize that no one and nothing can spite God, or go against His will. Everything happens in accordance with God's will, and it was only at His bidding that the wind carried out His mission."

# EXPLANATORY NOTES

*Words in small capitals within the text are explained in separate entries.*

ABRAHAM
Great patriarch and father of Isaac, traditionally considered the founder of the Hebrew nation as well as of the Arab tribes. Abraham was also father of ISHMAEL.

BADCHEN
A jester, entertainer, master of ceremonies at weddings and other Jewish festivities. A badchen is a balladeer, poet and composer all rolled into one. His compositions are usually extemporaneous. Badchens are not nearly as common and popular now as they were many years ago.

BAR MITZVAH

The celebration of a Jewish boy's coming of age, held in a SYNAGOGUE on a Saturday as close to a boy's actual thirteenth birthday as possible. The bar mitzvah boy reads a portion of the TORAH during the SABBATH service and sometimes makes a speech. After a boy is bar mitzvah, he can participate fully in all religious services.

CANTOR

A specially trained singer who participates with the RABBI in conducting religious services in the SYNAGOGUE or temple. The cantor sings long passages of the liturgy, in which he is sometimes joined by the congregants.

CHALLAH

The traditional loaf of bread baked for the SABBATH and other Jewish holy days. For the Sabbath the loaf is almost always shaped in a braid. At other times it may be round, oblong or even shaped like a ladder. The flavor of a challah is very special—the bread is soft and white and the crust is brown and very crisp.

CHANUKAH

Chanukah is a post-Biblical religious holiday. Usually celebrated in late November or December, it is also called the Festival of Lights, and lasts for eight days. Chanukah commemorates the rededication of the Temple in Jerusalem after the Maccabbees' victory over the Syrians, c. 165 B.C. For eight days Jews light small candles or oil in a special candleholder called a menorah. During Chanukah, gifts, often in the form of money, are given to children, special tops called dreidels are spun and special foods are eaten.

CHEDER

A one-room school where Hebrew and religious subjects were taught, particularly on the elementary level.

ELIJAH THE PROPHET

One of the most popular and best-loved figures in Jewish lore. Elijah is considered the protector of the poor and the defenseless. He is thought of as a miracle worker and most often depicted as appearing in disguise.

HASSID

Someone who follows the Hassidic way of life and religious beliefs. The Hassidic movement was founded in Europe in the eighteenth century by Israel ben Eliezer, who later became known as the Baal Shem-Tov. He said that God could be worshiped anywhere, not only in a SYNA-GOGUE, but also in an open field, at home, under a tree. He was critical of what he considered the formality and pedantry of religious practices of his time and advocated simple, happy, personal prayers, at times accompanied by dancing and singing.

In the story, "If Not Still Higher," the Rabbi of Nemirov is a Hassidic RABBI, who believed that doing a good deed during a special time of prayer was more important than praying in the synagogue. The LITVAK, with his pedantic, narrow-minded view of praying, represents the other side of the coin. The Litvak's conversion to the rabbi's views is a victory for Hassidism, a movement in which Peretz was very much interested. In fact, "If Not Still Higher" is only one of a series of Hassidic tales written by Peretz.

HAVDALA PRAYER

This prayer marks the end of the holy SABBATH or holiday, and is said over a cup of wine filled to overflowing. The overflowing cup is supposed to symbolize the coming of a full and prosperous week.

ISHMAEL

Son of Abraham; traditionally considered—by both Muslims and Jews—to be the founder of the Bedouin tribes.

KIDDUSH

The prayer of sanctification of the SABBATH or holiday. It is usually recited over a cup of wine at home or in the SYNAGOGUE. When wine is not available, the Kiddush prayer may be recited over CHALLAH.

LEVIATHAN

A legendary serpentlike creature that is supposed to encircle all the seas of the universe and whose wrath, if provoked, could destroy the world.

LITVAK

A nickname for a Jew who comes from Lithuania. A Litvak is supposed to be very learned in religious matters but pedantic, skeptical, shrewd and something of a know-it-all. The Lithuanian Jews of many years ago were strongly opposed to the Hassidic movement. (See HASSID.)

MATZOTH

Unleavened bread that looks like large crackers and is eaten during PASSOVER. The matzo is a reminder that during the Exodus Jews had to leave Egypt in such a hurry that they could not even wait for their bread to rise. (See also SEDER.)

### NEILAH

Neilah is the closing prayer recited as the sun begins to set on the afternoon of YOM KIPPUR. With this prayer everyone in the SYNAGOGUE can express his repentance and beg for God's forgiveness.

### PASSOVER

This eight-day holiday, celebrated in March or April, commemorates the deliverance of the Jews from Egypt some 3200 years ago, as told in the Book of Exodus in the Bible. (See also MATZOTH and SEDER.)

### PHYLACTERIES

Two small, black leather cubes with leather straps. These cubes contain small parchments on which four passages from the books of Exodus and Deuteronomy in the Bible are written. During morning prayers each day, except on the SABBATH and holy days, phylacteries are strapped in a special way on a man's forehead and left arm.

The custom of strapping on phylacteries comes from a commandment in the Book of Exodus which says: "It shall be a sign unto thee upon thine hand, and for a memorial between thine eyes, that the Lord's law may be in thy mouth." Traditionally, a bride-to-be should make a special, often elaborately embroidered bag for her future husband's phylacteries, just like the one made by the young girl in the story, "The Match."

### PURIM

This festival, celebrated in late February or March, commemorates the deliverance of Jews in Persia. Hamman, an evil adviser to the king of Persia, plotted to destroy all the Jews in the land, but his plot was thwarted by the king's Jewish wife, Esther, and by her cousin, Mordecai (commonly but incorrectly called her uncle).

The Book of Esther is read in the SYNAGOGUE on the eve and morning of Purim. Whenever Hamman's name is mentioned during the reading, everyone in the synagogue stomps his feet, hisses, jeers and even uses special noisemakers to drown out Hamman's name. Gifts of food and money are given to the poor, and delicious three-cornered pastries are eaten. All kinds of parties and masquerades are held at Purim time.

### RABBI

The word rabbi means "teacher." A rabbi, however, is not only a teacher and scholar, but also a specially trained and ordained person who is the chief religious official in a SYNAGOGUE or temple, and the authority concerning all rituals connected with Judaism.

### ROSH HASHANAH

One of the most revered of all Jewish holy days, celebrated in September, this marks the beginning of the Jewish New Year and is supposed to commemorate the creation of the world itself. Rosh Hashanah ushers in ten days of penitence, which end with the most important of all holy days, YOM KIPPUR. During this period of penitence,

Jews pray for forgiveness of sins and bad deeds committed against God and their fellow man.

### SABBATH

The Fourth Commandment says: "Six days thou shalt labor, and do all thy work, but on the seventh day is the Sabbath of the Lord, thy God." Pious Jews take a day of complete rest from labor and worries from sundown on Friday to sundown on Saturday. They pray to God, study the Holy Books and participate in discussions on all phases of Judaism. They may not run but only walk on the Sabbath, and there are limits set on how far they may walk.

During the time when Peretz wrote his stories, and even now in many Jewish homes, preparations for the Sabbath begin on Thursday. Food is brought home, the house is cleaned from top to bottom, fresh clothing is prepared, everyone bathes and gets ready to greet the Sabbath.

Just before sundown on Friday, women light Sabbath candles and recite special prayers over them. Two covered CHALLAHS are put on the table and delicious foods are served. When the father returns from SYNAGOGUE, he blesses his children, sings hymns in praise of his wife and then recites the KIDDUSH over a cup of wine.

Traditionally, Jews invite a guest for the Sabbath meal —a poor or homeless person, a penniless student or someone far away from home. To bring a guest home is to honor the Sabbath as well as to do a good deed.

### SABBATH GENTILE

A non-Jewish person who performs such chores as opening ovens, putting out or lighting fires and other tasks for Jews on the holy SABBATH. A gentile person has to be asked to perform these tasks before the start of Sabbath. It is a sin for a Jew even to *ask* anyone to perform work on the Sabbath.

### SARAH BATH TUVIM

A legendary figure in Jewish folklore, beloved by women, especially in the days when Peretz wrote his stories. Sarah Bath Tuvim is presumed to have been a real person, the daughter and granddaughter of RABBIS who lived in the Lithuanian town of Brisk in the seventeenth or eighteenth century.

It is thought that Sarah Bath Tuvim must have had a particularly difficult life. She poured out her thoughts and feelings in moving prayers which were written not only with great emotion, but with grace and poetic beauty. These are not formal SYNAGOGUE prayers but informal pleas to God, and are preserved to this day in Jewish folk literature. Sarah Bath Tuvim's prayers are considered essentially women's prayers, as she herself was considered a special heroine by Jewish women in Peretz's time.

### SEDER

A gathering of family and friends for a feast on the first and second nights of PASSOVER. A special book called a Haggadah is read during the Seder service. This book tells the story of the Exodus of the Jews from Egypt. It also contains comments on the story, as well as songs, hymns and questions and answers.

No leavening, such as yeast or baking powder, can be

used in Passover foods, nor can leavening ever have come in contact with any Passover dishes or utensils, so MATZOTH are eaten and special dishes and utensils are used. During the Seder bitter herbs, commemorating the bitterness of slavery, are served. Also on the table are a paste made of nuts, wine, apples and cinnamon, symbolizing the clay from which Jews made bricks in the days of slavery, and a bone and roasted egg, signifying offerings brought to the Temple in ancient Jerusalem. The man leading the Seder service sits in an easy chair, or is propped up by pillows, to show his sense of ease and well-being in contrast to slavery.

### SHAVUOTH

This two-day holiday, observed in May or June, celebrates the covenant that was made between God and the Israelites on Mount Sinai. Shavuoth is also called "The Giving to Us of the TORAH on Mount Sinai."

### "SHEMA ISRAEL" PRAYER

This is the central prayer of the Jewish people and is the first prayer taught to Jewish children. It confirms that Jews accept the principle and the authority imposed on them by the Kingdom of Heaven. The full text of the Shema is composed of three paragraphs, each of them affirming the Jews' faith and love for God. It is recited upon rising, at evening prayers and just before going to sleep.

### SHIVAH

Seven days of mourning for someone who has died. These days begin immediately after the funeral. Close relatives sit on low stools in the home of the person who died. Friends and neighbors come to pay their respects and to bring food, help and comfort to the mourners.

### SHOCHET

Shochet means a kosher butcher or slaughterer, and kosher means fit to be eaten according to Jewish dietary laws. The kosher laws require certain ways of slaughtering, and forbid the eating of certain foods such as pork and shellfish and the mixing of meat and dairy foods. A shochet is trained to slaughter animals in accordance with Jewish ritual. He must be a person of good health, mental alertness, piety and pure character. His work is supervised by a RABBI.

### SIMCHATH TORAH

In Hebrew these words mean "the day of rejoicing in the TORAH." This holy day, observed on the final day of SUC-COTH, is a very happy one, with singing and dancing in the SYNAGOGUE. It celebrates the completion of a full year's reading of the entire Torah in the synagogue. When the last chapter of Deuteronomy is read, the first chapter of Genesis immediately follows. This indicates that the study of Torah is a never-ending cycle for Jews everywhere.

### SLICHOTH

The word Slichoth means forgiveness and is used to describe penitential prayers. The recital of Slichoth prayers begins during the week preceding ROSH HASHANAH and continues until YOM KIPPUR.

STAR OF DAVID

A six-pointed star symbolizing Judaism.

SUCCOTH

In October the Festival of Tabernacles, as Succoth is also called, celebrates the fall harvest and commemorates the time after the Exodus from Egypt when Jews wandered in the wilderness and lived in huts. A special hut or booth, called a succah, is built out of doors, on rooftops, in back-yards or on balconies. The succah is covered with tree branches and decorated with flowers, fruits, nuts and leaves. Pious Jews eat in the succah throughout the week-long Succoth holiday.

SYNAGOGUE

A Jewish house of worship, which always includes a study hall because prayer and study must go on hand-in-hand. Sometimes a synagogue is also called a temple.

TALMUD

An enormously large collection of commentaries, debates, discussions and conclusions interpreting the TORAH. The Talmud consists of two parts. The first part, called the Mishnah, is the interpretation of Biblical laws. The second part, called the Gemara, is a collection of commentaries on the Mishnah.

TORAH

The Torah is considered the holiest of all scriptures in Judaism. It consists of the Five Books of Moses: Genesis, Exodus, Leviticus, Numbers and Deuteronomy. The Torah must be written by hand, with a quill and special ink, on special parchment by a specially trained scribe. It is read aloud in the SYNAGOGUE on the SABBATH, all holy days, and on Mondays and Thursdays. The Torah is divided into weekly sections, and the reading of the whole is completed during the course of a year. (Also see SIMCHATH TORAH.)

TZADDIK

A holy and righteous man, often thought to have supernatural powers of healing. Some Jews believe that a tzaddik can perform miracles and that he can even speak directly to God.

YIDDISH

A language spoken by Jews all over the world. It originated in eastern Europe and is almost one thousand years old. Jews call it their "mother tongue." Yiddish is an exceptionally rich and expressive language. It is also very idiomatic, and includes many words from other languages, particularly from German and Hebrew. In fact, Yiddish includes words from all the languages in all the countries where Jews live. It uses the Hebrew alphabet and is written from right to left.

YOM KIPPUR

Yom Kippur, also called the Day of Atonement, is observed ten days after ROSH HASHANAH, in September or October. It is marked by a twenty-four-hour fast, and by day-long prayers in the temple or SYNAGOGUE. Yom Kippur ends the ten days of penitence which begin with ROSH HASHANAH. (See also NEILAH.) Throughout this holiest of all days in the Hebrew calendar, Jews everywhere pray for forgiveness of sins and bad deeds committed against God and their fellow man.